True Ghost Stories

Frightening Accounts of Haunted Houses,
Paranormal Mysteries, and Unexplained
Phenomenon

Selinda Hart

True Ghost Stories

Frightening Accounts of Haunted Houses, Paranormal Mysteries, and Unexplained Phenomenon

Selinda Hart

ISBN 978-0692434291

Table of Contents

Introduction   v

Something In The Dark   1

Something In The Dark, Part 2   5

Haunted School   11

The House Off Greenville   17

Ghostly Passenger   25

Red Balloon   31

Dark Of The Woods   41

Haunted Town   49

Ghost In The Bedroom   57

The Landscape Ghost   69

Night Visitor   73

Agnes   79

Birthday Surprise   87

Who's Been Playing With My Kids?   93

Hotel Ghost   101

Cliff Of Darkness   111

About the Author   121

Introduction

"RUE GHOST STOR*IES*" *IS A*

Tollection of real and frightening paranormal accounts based on real people who lived to tell about them. Each story is unique in its own personal experience and has been told to me, Selinda Hart. Having worked as an investigator and as a researcher for the paranormal radio show "Tia Maria" I have brought together some of the best hauntings, paranormal accounts and true stories in my first collection. The sixteen stories in this book, include diverse paranormal phenomena and unexplained mysteries set in different locations in the United States, and one compelling frightening story from Spain. As one former skeptic recants from his scary experience, "I was never a believer in the paranormal and I thought ghosts were simply a figment of someone's over-active imagination. I no longer scoff at people who claim to see ghosts. I never found out who or what was haunting that house. But I wasn't going to stay and find out."

"The House off Greenville," "Red Balloon," "Ghost in the Bedroom," and "Who's been playing with my kids?" are real stories about events and paranormal activit that took place in the Dallas house I lived in as a single mom for over five years. My children are grown now, but to this day they do not like talking about the strange activity and events that took place in that house. If you enjoy reading scary stories, paranormal mysteries and unexplained phenomena, then "True Ghost Stories" will leave you with chills. So get comfortable, snuggle up, and get under the covers. Let me tell you a story···

Something In The Dark

IALL STARTED WHEN **I** WAS 12 years old. I wasn't aware of the strange happenings right away but I remember when my parents moved my sister, brother and I into my grandparent's old house, the hauntings began. Due to hardship and a series of unfortunate events at the time, we suddenly found ourselves homeless. Thankfully, my grandparents took us in. At first, the sudden move seemed like an adventure. The house sat on a sprawling five acres of land in beautiful Montana. But deep inside myself, I knew there was something not right about my grandparent's house. It wasn't anything you could put your finger on. The best way to describe it is "a feeling of dread." I tried to dismiss it to the strangeness and uneasiness of my new surroundings. After all, this was an old house. But eventually the feeling of dread and the thickness in the air became overwhelming.

As time went by, our mother started to act strange. She had always been a loving mother to us and had a wonderful sense of humor, she would often joke with us. In the months since our move, she began to change. She would unexpectedly fly off the handle over nothing. It was like she was so angry all the time. Instead of her usual loving self, she was always drained, sick or angry. One time she went to visit my older sister in South Carolina. She stayed with her for a few months. As soon as she was away from the old house, she was back to normal and was herself again. It was as if something in the house would influence her personality or possess her.

One night my sister and I were laying on our bed in the dark. It was very late and everyone in the house was asleep. My mom had gone to stay with my older sister for a few weeks. We whispered in the night, confiding our worries, our dreams, and our fears to one another.

"Mom is so different in this house." I told her.

"I know," she murmured. "She has changed, it's like she's another person."

We snuggled in bed and found refuge and comfort in each other's arms. Across the room a creak interrupted our conversation. The bedroom door gradually opened. A dark figure was standing in the doorway.

"Who is it?" I stammered.

There was no answer. I couldn't make out any distinct features except for one, a set of menacing red eyes. They pierced through the darkness. My sister and I stared in disbelief at the entrance. Then, we heard it, a very low creepy laugh. My heart started to pound. Then without warning, the dark figure disappeared. My sister and I stared for what seemed like several seconds before anyone spoke. Finally, I got up. We assumed it was our brother trying to mess with us. We rushed to the doorway, but there was nothing there.

Our brother slept at the far end of the house so I knew he couldn't have gone down the hallway without us hearing him. I tiptoed to my brother's room as quickly as I could. He was sound asleep. Later in our room we tried to convince ourselves our eyes were playing tricks on us. Secretly we knew that we both had seen something we couldn't explain. Eventually we fell sleep, but after several minutes, I felt something sitting on my feet. The pressure woke me up. When I tried to move my feet, I couldn't. I cried out and startled my sister awake. She screamed and the sensation stopped.

"There was something dark sitting on your bed watching you!" she shouted.

I don't know what was sitting on my bed that night. I never did find out, but what I do know is that it was evil. There were many paranormal events over the years in that house. I am now grown with children of my own. My parents later moved into a house they built on my grandparents land. The hauntings continued.

Something In The Dark, Part 2

AT 17, **I** HAD MOVED OUT OF MY parent's house and was on my own. The strange and creepy paranormal experiences my sister and I had endured as children in that house were in my past, and I suppressed them until they were almost forgotten. A few years later, I was married and the mother of two small children. My parents built a small home on their property. It was next door to their house, but with enough distance that we had our own place and privacy. There were plenty of acres with lots of trees on the land. It seemed like an idyllic place to raise children with lots of space for my beautiful Labrador. We moved in. My husband started working late at night and I was often left alone with my kids. Thankfully my dog kept me company.

One night, I heard whimpering outside my door.

"Come on girl, come inside." I opened the door to call her to my bedside. She sat motionless outside my room.

"What's the matter?"

I noticed she never entered my room by herself. She often had to be led through the door and had the habit of resisting. I called her again, but she wouldn't budge. Finally after several attempts at coaxing her, I pulled her through the doorway and into the room. She lay on my bed as I stroked her soft fur. Something captured her attention. She looked in the direction of my closet with a blank stare. I shut the bedroom door and plopped on the bed. She continued to gaze at the closet door for a very long time. She did not waver but obediently stayed by my side.

"What's the matter girl?" Then I heard it, a noise coming from outside my room. The door creaked. Slowly it began to open and with every inch, my heart raced. My husband walked in.

'Oh it's you,' I sighed with relief.

'What's she looking at?' My husband asked with curiosity.

'I don't know she's been staring at that corner for an hour.'

We finally settled for bed and we were beginning to doze off when she got restless and started to whimper.

'I need to get some sleep,' my husband complained under his breath. He got up to put her outside.

Sometime during the night, I awoke from a stinging pain on my right leg. Something had scratched me. At first I thought it was my dog. Then I remembered, she wasn't in the room. I got up to turn on the bathroom light and saw **three** long red marks running down my thigh.

"What?" I couldn't explain the scratches. I turned off the light before going back to bed. It waslate, but I forced myself back to sleep. Later that night I felt a deep, heavy pressure on my chest. I couldn'tbreathe. I started to gasp for air; it felt as if I was beingsuffocated. When I opened my eyes, I couldn't move. My body was paralyzed; someone or something washolding me in place.

Then I heard it, the sinister low creepy laugh, one I was all too familiar with from my childhood. It was the evil laugh from the entity that terrified us when we lived in the house next door.

"Ha ha ha ha," the laughter was maniacal followed by heavy breathing on my face.

I could only move my hand that was right by my husband and I started hitting him until he finally woke up. He sat up startled. I was finally able to breathe. What-ever it was, released me from his grip. I coughed and coughed and eventually caught mybreath. My husband was catatonic. He stared at thecorner of the room. I turned in the direction he waslooking. We sat frozen in disbelief. There, next to thecloset in the corner of our bedroom was an ominousfigure.

Through the darkness of the room, we could see it, blacker than the night. But what was it? His red eyes pierced right at us. Then I remembered and I knew. It was the same menacing dark evil figure that frightened my sister and I as children. It stared at me and tore the stillness of the night with a low guttural evil laugh as if to say "welcome back."

According to A. Morrison's paranormal account told to Selinda Hart, "geologically our home falls on lay lines and Native American grounds. Our family property in Montana, I discovered is within the boundaries of the Salish and Kootenai tribes. I do believe there is a direct correlation to all the paranormal activity and unexplained phenomena we experienced. After several years, our family finally moved away. The spiritual activity had become far too frequent and an overwhelming burden on all of us. I often felt attacked and my husband had experienced a spiritual attachment and began to suffer physical ailments. I found out later that other people living on the same road had also experienced spiritual trauma."

Haunted School

I HAD BEEN ASSIGNED TO A SCHOOL in the Carrollton Farmers Branch Independent School District that was located less than a mile from a small 200 year old cemetery on the hill. As a brand new teacher, I often stayed late organizing and preparing lessons for the following day. Usually I was left alone in the building, long after other teachers had gone home. But I liked the quiet hallways and working late into the evening. Except for the custodian, I was completely by myself at school. One night, the custodian came to my door.

"Ms. T did you need something? I saw that you pressed the emergency button in the gym."

Puzzled, I told him I hadn't gone to the gym and although I appreciated his concern, I reassured him that I hadn't called for help. He looked a little pale and looked at me with a funny expression on his face.

"Maybe some kids got inside and are playing in the gym," I told him.

"There is no one in the building," he said abruptly.

Then he turned around and quickly walked down the hall into one of the classrooms to finish cleaning. I thought it was odd that he hadn't gone to check. Curious, I walked a few feet towards the gymnasium and opened the heavy doors. It was dark but I could hear whispers at the back of the gym wall. As soon as the door opened unexpectedly, it sounded like students had scampered to hide. There was a basketball rolling on the floor toward my feet. I tried to flip on the light switch by the front entrance, but the lights didn't work. I left the door open, and walked inside. I spotted the emergency intercom button, on the adjacent wall. It was pushed down. Someone had called from the gym. To my surprise, the air felt a little thick and musty and it was unusually cold inside. But, stranger still was the feeling that someone was watching me from the back of the gym.

"Hello, who is there?" My voice echoed in the stillness of the vast room.

For some reason I was compelled to walk further inside to investigate. I went to the restrooms to make sure there wasn't anyone hiding or playing inside. I flipped the light switch on but the lights didn't work in either of the restrooms. They were empty and unoccupied. Suddenly the gym door slammed shut with a loud metal noise. It startled me and I jumped. Only the outside streetlight emitted partial illumination through the window openings just below the ceiling. As I made my way back to the entrance, I heard footsteps. Every time I took a step, I could hear the sound of someone walking following close behind. My eyes adjusted to the darkness and by one of the gym walls I could make out the shadows of two boys.

"What are you doing here?" I asked. "Don't you know it's after hours? You need to go home," I scolded them.

My high heel shoes clicked and echoed in the large space and high ceiling of the gymnasium. As I approached the back wall and got closer, the shadows of the boys seemed to evaporate into thin air. I was stunned. I stood staring at the walls and the empty gym. Could my eyes have been playing tricks on me? No, I definitely saw two boys standing at the back wall. What about the whispers? I know I had heard whispers, and footsteps.

The next day, I told another teacher what had happened to me the night before at school. She was quiet for a moment and then explained that several years ago there had been an accident at the school. According to her, there were a couple of students who had sneaked into the gym after hours to shoot baskets.

"Nobody knows how the fire started. People thought it was an electrical accident due to faulty wiring. The smoke filled the gym quickly, but the doors had gotten stuck and they couldn't get out. The boys trapped inside the gym, perished," she sighed.

We remained quiet for a while. Then she looked at me as if remembering something.

"They are buried at the nearby cemetery just down the road. I guess their ghosts still come to play."

Her experience told personally to Selinda Hart left Miss T rattled, but she continued teaching in CFBISD and at her haunted school for a few more years before becoming an Assistant Principal at another school district.

The House
Off Greenville

S EVERAL YEARS AGO, I MOVED into a two story house in Dallas close to an old part of town, near fashionable and trendy Greenville Avenue. The house sat on a corner close to the famous "M" streets. It was early summer and the trees were green and overprotective. I remember thinking I had to quickly find an apartment or house for rent. My husband and I had recently divorced and for the first time in my life I was on my own. Feeling a sense of adventure and independence, I began looking for a house to rent for my two young children and me. Driving around alone, I had taken an unexpected turn off Greenville and found myself lost in a lovely old neighborhood of manicured lawns and lovely gardens. I came to a corner trying to figure out where I was, and recognized the area as one of the most coveted in Dallas. Certain that the houses were out of my price range even for a rental, I tried to find my way out. But something got my attention.

As if on cue, a yellow brick house sitting on that very same corner to my right had a "for rent" sign on the yard in front of a big maple tree. It was as if the house itself had called me. Without thinking, I got out of my car and walked up surreptitiously over the cracked sidewalk where the branches hovered over the porch welcoming me. To my surprise the front door was open, "Hello," I called out. Immediately, I noticed the beautiful wooden floors, the pretty peach colored walls in the front room with a large Spanish arch that separated the living room from the dining room. A noise from one of the bedrooms startled me and I quickly realized I wasn't alone. "Hello?" My voice seemed to reverberate in echo on the empty walls. I approached the back room with some trepidation and to my relief it was a man in work clothes painting the master bedroom. I apologized profusely, telling him I noticed a sign in the front yard and confessed I had let myself inside. The painter, who introduced himself as Jose said the owner was renting the house and had just placed the sign outside only moments before. I soon discovered the rent was quite reasonable. What luck!

In a short time, I moved to this beautiful old house, rearranged the furniture and my life. It took a couple of months before I felt at home in my pretty brick house on the corner of Homer Street with the crooked sidewalk. I don't remember exactly when I first noticed my home was a little strange. Maybe it was the trees outside that made menacing dancing shadows at night in my bedroom or perhaps it was the hallway. The walls were painted in an odd almost sinister dark bluish black shade. I often wondered, why would anyone want to paint the hallway that color? Every time I walked through the hallway toward one of the bedrooms, the air would get unusually heavy. Whenever I felt that uneasy feeling, I chalked it up to not being use to my new surroundings. My small children lived with me and shared a room at the other end of the hallway.

One late afternoon when they were spending the weekend with their father, I took advantage of catching up with house chores and later relaxed on the coach to read a book. It must have been around three o'clock in the afternoon. I was feeling tired and eventually my eyelids got so heavy, I decided to take a nap. As I walked through the hallway in the direction of my bedroom, I felt an unexpected tug on the back of my shirt. For a moment, I thought my shirt had gotten stuck on something and I turned around. The sensation felt as if a small child had pulled my shirt from my lower back. After a quick look around me, I saw nothing in the dark hallway that could have caught my shirt. Except for the low grey futon with a wine stain, something I had kept from the divorce, the hallway was empty.

Feeling sleepy, I yawned to myself and didn't think twice about it. Once on my bed, I dozed off into a very deep sleep. It must have been hours later, when I began to hear the music. I don't know how long I had slept, but it was evening and my bedroom was pitch dark. Only the outside streetlight offered a bit of lighting. The furniture in my room was in shadows and I intermittently blinked open and closed my eyes again. Why was I so overwhelmingly listless? It was difficult to open my eyes for too long and easily gave in to more sleep and lay there in the darkness of the room.

I think it was the music, a smooth jazzy instrumental piece from the 1960's that first woke me up. I didn't recognize the tune, but I could clearly hear the music played somewhere nearby. The Greenville house sat in a corner and it wasn't unusual for cars with the radio blaring, to pass by from time to time. The side street of Homer was often used to cut across to the Central Expressway access road or to the busier Fitzhugh Avenue a couple of blocks away. The music was coming from someone walking by on the sidewalk or coming from a car playing "oldies" on the radio. The music continued playing and when I realized it did not fade as one might expect from a passing car, I decided it must be coming from next door.

A little groggy, I lifted my head momentarily from the pillow with my eyes closed and the music suddenly stopped as if someone had lifted the needle from an old record player. I stayed sitting up for a few seconds and decided against getting up and plopped my head back down on my pillow. The music started to play again. "No," I thought to myself, "it must be someone outside with a radio." In a half wake state, I sat upright again holding myself up with my elbows, and just as I did, the music stopped. My body felt very heavy and I decided to give in to slumber once again, allowing my head to hit the pillow with a thud. The strange thing was my body felt completely drained of energy. As soon as my head rested, the music would play again and every time I lifted my head from the pillow, the music stopped. Then in my sleeplike stupor, I blinked and managed to force my eyes open.

Something strange was going on and I wasn't dreaming. I could clearly make out voices, people laughing and talking to one another. It sounded like a roomful of guests, a party. Then to my alarm, I realized the music, the party noises, and the voices were not coming from next door or from outside. They were coming from inside my house! For a few seconds I just lay there. I was wide awake by now and didn't know what to do. Gradually I sat up and could still hear the voices and instrumental music coming from the living and dining room area. I swallowed hard, eventually gathering enough courage to get up from my bed to investigate. As I tiptoed through the hallway and approached the front rooms, the music and the voices faded mysteriously. As I got closer, the music and the voices stopped completely. I was standing in the middle of the living room alone in the dark. It was deadly silent and there was no one in my house. Or was there?

"Several strange incidents occurred at that house off Greenville and over the next five years, I experienced unexplained paranormal activity. I eventually came to the realization I was not alone. There were other ghostly occupants in the house living with me." (Selinda Hart)

Ghostly Passenger

WAS MANY YEARS AGO WHEN I was a young sixteen year old living on Murray street in San Antonio. The year was 1944 and my three older brothers were in the army stationed in Europe during WWII. Being the youngest I was too young to serve at the time, so I lived with my parents. Not too many teenagers had cars back then, besides everyone pretty much walked where they needed to go in those days. I was use to walking a lot, to school, town or wherever my mom or my dad sent me to run errands. If I ever needed to travel pretty far, I'd simply take the bus.

I had been doing odd jobs around town and worked for my father at the tailor shop after school. Finally, I was making a little bit of money and started to save for a car. What was my motivation? I wanted to start dating and be able to take girls to school dances. Borrowing my dad's car was not an option especially since he needed it for work. One night I lay in bed, calculating how much more I had to save in order to afford a car. Then I remembered there was a used car lot on Commerce Street, not far from the "Malt House."

It was a crisp October night very late around 2:00 in the morning and there were hardly any cars driving on the normally busy street. I could usually hear cars driving by especially when I had the window to my room open. Murray Street was off Commerce and our small white house was a couple of homes down from the busy intersection. I slipped out of the window of my bedroom without my dad finding out and crossed the main street and strolled to the used car lot to see what they were selling. There weren't too many lights on the lot but I could make out the latest models even in the shadows. Thankfully, there was a big full moon that night and by the light of the moon, I'd peek inside several cars to see the interiors and scope out the prices.

The cars lined up at the front were usually the ones in better condition but also the most expensive. Then from the distance on the back row I saw it, a black shiny beauty. It was parked apart from the rest of the vehicles. "Hmmm, they probably just got this one," I thought to myself. I made a beeline and walked towards the brand new looking Chevy. The moonlight gave the car an alluring sheen. I admired the car from all angles and even kicked a tire or two.

When I saw the price on the card sitting on the base of the windshield, I couldn't believe it. It wasn't expensive at all! Maybe my dream of owning my own car would come true after all. I could actually afford this one and it didn't look like a used car. I patted the hood as if it was already mine and made a plan to go by the lot the following day. By now it was around 2:30 in the morning and there weren't any cars passing by on Commerce Street.

People in the neighborhood were probably asleep and everything was quiet. I knew I'd have to get home and sneak in so as not to wake up my mom or dad. But I thought I'd give the car one last look. I peered inside the driver's side of the window but couldn't see very well and for some strange reason, there seemed to be a package or something on the passenger's side. I walked around the front of the car to get a closer look. I looked at the interior and could make out the front seats and the dashboard. The car looked like it was in mint condition. I cupped my hands on the window to get a better look with my face glued to the passenger window. Gradually the outline of a man's face began to appear right before me. Staring back at me at close range was a pair of eyes!

I fell back several feet hitting the pavement, I was so startled. This was not my reflection and after a few seconds with my heart pounding out of my chest, I finally mustered the courage and slowly approached the car once again. As I got close to the window I felt fearful but was compelled to cup my hands and look inside the vehicle once more to make sure my eyes had not played tricks on me. My heart pounded so hard and I forced myself to peer inside the window, but I could see there was nothing. I pulled away from the vehicle and got a real creepy feeling, "what had I just seen?"

The next day in the light of day, I went to the lot and noticed the car was gone. "Hey, what happened to the black Chevy on the last row?" I asked Floyd, a mechanic at the lot. He shook his head from side to side and said bluntly, "you don't want that car." I Insisted, I had enough money and could pay for it with cash. He stared at me gravely snapping his lips in disapproval.

"Don't you know someone was found dead in that car?" My heart almost stopped.

"What?" I asked him. He told me a story that leaves me cold to this day. He said a few years earlier, a man had been found dead and his body was found in the passenger's seat with his eyes wide open.

"The police found him on the side of the road a few miles out of town, they don't know what happened to him, he wasn't very old, but had died right there inside the car. According to the cops, they didn't find any foul play. It's strange though, they could never solve the mystery either. Funny thing too, no one has been able to keep the car for very long. Oh, there is always a customer. I mean, they'll buy it and then after just a few weeks or a month or so, the car is returned to the lot."

Floyd said it in a matter of fact demeanor as he wiped his hands on a rag. Standing there as if I had been sucker punched, I scratched my head confused and stunned. I've asked myself time and time again, did I see a ghost? That was many years ago when I had that awful experience and the image of what I saw that night stayed with me all my life. I've never forgotten the ghostly passenger.

Rudy Reyna personally shared with me his frightening paranormal account as he experienced it when he was a teenager. He told it to me many years ago. It was a creepy tale I heard over the years and more than a few times. Mr. Reyna never deviated from the details and events of the story as they unfolded that night. According to Mr. Reyna this is a true story and the memory of the ghostly passenger haunted him.

Red Balloon

WE HAD SETTLED **I**N A CORNER yellow brick house off Greenville Avenue at the end of summer. My children were very young at the time and as a single mom, I did everything I could to make the big move as comfortable as possible. I don't remember exactly when I first noticed strange things about my home. There were creaks and unusual sounds but I quickly dismissed them as part of the house settling. After all, the two story structure was built in the 1930's. The house had an interesting floor plan with the kitchen at the back, behind the dining room. There was a door from the kitchen area that led to the back yard where my children often played for hours.

The incessant downpour kept them inside this one particular Saturday morning. Cleaning my little kitchen and charming nook was something I had put off, but on this rainy day it seemed like the perfect time to do it, I had already run out of excuses. I lined up my household items and sprays and placed them on the circular glass table to take on the project of making my little kitchen sparkle or at least remove the dingy yellow stains that never seemed to come off the old tile floor.

My children played with little dolls and action figures in their room. "Mom" I heard one of them call me a few minutes later. I was on my knees scrubbing the grime from the faded tiles and the embedded dirt between their art deco design. "Mom" I heard the voice again. I knew they were calling for snacks and I got up and walked down the hallway and stood at their bedroom entrance. "What?" I asked. Both my kids turned to me puzzled. "What?" I asked them again as they stared at me with a funny look on their face. They were lost in a game of dolls and scattered Legos on the floor.

"We didn't call you mommy" Karen said. Jimmy shook his head "no" and looked up at me.

"Well, somebody called me, I heard you from the kitchen." They had a wide eyed look and both shrugged their shoulders, then they continued playing.

I walked back to the kitchen and to my housework. "Hmmm", I said under my breath somewhat disgruntled. "I know I didn't imagine it, somebody called me."

As the last week of September approached, I got ready to celebrate my son Jimmy's 4th birthday. The invitations had been sent and everything was ready at a nearby pizza place where there were plenty of games for all the children. My son had received many gifts that day, but the one he took the most interest in was a simple red balloon given to him at the party. Late in the evening at home, my children were still in a playful mood and they chattered endlessly in my bedroom. Still excited from the party, my children were laughing and running around the house. I could hear them calling to the red helium balloon beckoning it to follow them. It floated in the air as they called to it, "Over here, over here" and they laughed, delighted as the balloon seemed to follow their every move. I didn't think much about it, until they returned to my bedroom.

It had been an unusually hot Texas night and I had the window air conditioner running full blast. Despite the fact that it was an old unit, it blew powerful gusts of air directly towards the entrance of the room. The kids often stood in front of the unit to let their hair blow wildly or to hear their voices vibrate in unison. As the children bustled back into my room and called to the balloon, it seemed to hover in the hallway for a few seconds with its long string dangling by the doorway.

"Over here, over here, follow me, follow me" they begged giggling from inside the bedroom. I watched and smiled to myself at their amusement. The air conditioner was a clunky old, but powerful unit and I knew it was impossible for the balloon to re-enter the room. Suddenly the balloon wavered a bit and defying physics descended slightly from the ceiling in the hallway and adjusted itself to enter under the door frame and into the bedroom. I sat upright in disbelief and my blood went cold, not sure what I had just witnessed.

I didn't say a word to my children, as I was dumbfounded not being able to logically explain to myself what I had just seen. This was a strange happening and I too, followed the balloon's every move with my own eyes. I watched my kids as they played tag with the red balloon taunting it to chase them, "over here, over here!" They ran out of my bedroom and to my surprise, the balloon followed them throughout the house in every room they entered. It was as if someone or something held the end of the balloon string and followed my children's every move.

Later we got ready for bed and the discarded balloon floated aimlessly in the children's room by the toy boxes and shelves. Tired from all the activities and excitement of a long day, I fell on the comforter of my bed sprawled in exhaustion. I nudged my sleeping son.

"Go to your room Jimmy, you have to sleep in your bed."

My son often liked to sneak into my bed in the middle of the night and snuggle with me. My daughter had already taken her place in the top bunk of her room and was resting. A few minutes had passed when I heard my daughter's scream.

"Mom⋯Make it stop, make it stop!"

I ran as fast as I could to her room. I stopped in my tracks when I saw the red balloon floating in circles, circulating very fast and aggressively above her head around and around, as if begging her to play. It flew in a counter clock direction over her head in small continuous circles. She lay in bed with her blanket almost hiding her face in tears. I stared at the balloon in shock for a few seconds at the strange sight, then ran and grabbed the string and tied it to the bedroom door knob.

"Karen," I tried to soothe her, "it's ok, look the balloon is tied down. It's not floating; it won't fly around anymore. Don't be scared."

I didn't know how to explain the strange phenomenon especially since I had automatically reacted in mother bear protective mode to comfort my daughter. I suppose I was in denial at what I had just witnessed, not sure if I had a reasonable explanation. She peeked from her blanket and gradually lifted her head from her pillow. She seemed to settle down as soon as she saw the balloon secured and tied around the doorknob at the entrance. Slowly and cautiously, she got up and walked down the ladder from her top bunk to check for herself.

"Karen go brush your teeth, honey and go to sleep, it's late."

It was a few minutes later when I made my way back to my room and sat on the edge of my bed, about to get under the covers when I heard my daughter again. As my daughter climbed up the small ladder that led to the top bunk, I heard her scamper almost tripping over herself on the wooden floor. I heard her little bare feet as she ran to my room upset.

"Mommy···mommy!" She screamed and held me tight around my waist, "Mommy someone is in Jimmy's bed!"

My heart pounded fast in my chest as I ran towards her room wondering if I was going to confront an intruder? I peered from the hallway by the door, and quickly turned on the light to her room. There was no one. I glanced down at my daughter who stood behind me, her face buried in my blue robe. I pointed to my son's bunk bed.

"Karen, there isn't anyone on Jimmy's bed, look for yourself."

I tried to get her to see that his bunk bed was unoccupied but she wouldn't budge. She held on to my waist as tight as she could and looked momentarily in the direction of her brother's bunk bed and kept pointing as if she could see something.

"He's still there" she mumbled in my robe.

Later in my room after I had calmed her down, she told me in detail what happened. Karen said as she climbed up to her bed, she could see through the rungs of the ladder and into the bottom bunk below.

"A little boy was asleep in Jimmy's bed," she said. She stared for several seconds thinking it was her brother and when she realized a stranger was in his bed, she ran out of her room afraid. She described a small boy of about four or five years old dressed in a little jumper or pants with suspenders.

"His hair was like Jimmy's. His bangs came down on his forehead. But it wasn't Jimmy because he had blond hair."

Karen positioned herself in a fetal position placing her hand under her head to show how he was sleeping. I listened quietly and knew for a fact my son Jimmy had fallen asleep earlier in my bed and was still laying there, so I knew it wasn't him.

"The strangest thing of all mom, is I could see right through him."

Her eyes were as big as saucers and she was shaking as she relayed the story. She was telling the truth. I tried to pacify my daughter with hugs and kisses and soothe her to sleep. I didn't know what to think or what to say to appease her anxiety. Needless to say, we all slept in my bed that night, but this would not be the last of the little boy ghost. There would be more paranormal events in this strange house in the months and years we lived there. I still wonder to this day, who was playing with my kids? It was evident to me that on this night, my children had been playing with a ghost!

"The paranormal activity and unexplained phenomena continued at the house off Greenville while we lived there. My daughter Karen continued to see ghosts and entities over the next few years. She was a little girl at the time, but says she still remembers many strange things." According to her, *"some of the memories are still too frightening to talk about." (Selinda Hart)*

Dark
Of The Woods

WE HAD BEEN DR**I**V**I**NG FOR several miles through some winding roads when dusk descended. "Are you sure you are going the right way?" I asked. It was a cold February evening and the many bare branches of the woods accented the winter scene. My boyfriend and I had decided on a spontaneous road trip and after the long drive, we were ready to have a quiet dinner and relax in our cabin. The snow was beautiful and we witnessed deer scampering across the way. I had looked forward to getting away for a weekend in the woods of Colorado. The cabin site was remote and romantic and after hours of sitting in the car and seeing nothing but the icy road, we finally arrived to the beautiful "Sawmill Point Lodge."

We eagerly stretched our legs and made our way to our private cabin and began to unpack our gear. We were hungry and quickly settled in to unwind from our long journey. We sat in front of a cozy fireplace after supper. The cabin had beautiful wooden floors with a thick rug strategically placed close to the fireplace where we lay. But eventually my adventurous spirit got the best of me and I wanted to venture out and see the frozen lake. My boyfriend said flatly he didn't want to go out again into the cold night air. Miffed at his disinterest in observing the sights with me, I stormed out of the cabin alone.

It was midnight and the full moon cast long shadows in the snow as I walked through the woods toward the frozen lake leaving footprints behind me. There were mostly pine trees, but many other trees in the woods were tall and bare and the moonlight only enhanced the tall thin shadows above the night sky like twisted arms above me. Finally after walking several yards, I could make out the **froz**en lovely lake. I came to the edge, and the mirror looking floor made me want to step on it or at least place a toe to see if the ice on the surface was deep.

Suddenly something moving in the woods behind me got my attention. I turned around for amoment, but all I could see were a cluster of trees andbushes. I was sure I had heard someone chuckling,but I couldn't see anything. There was something strange in the air and I sensed someone watching me from behind the tall trees. I gazed across the lake andspotted a few lights from the scattered cabins that outlined the area. Only the reflection of the moon on the lake and snow was visible. Soft sounds of someone walking in the distance could beheard. Perhaps someone had decided on a moonlight walk into the woods to take in the winter night. Everything was lovely and deadly quiet.

The only thing I could hear were footsteps or something treading in the snow coming in the direction from the dark of the woods. I thought itmight be deer or an animal hunting for food. The feeling of being watched however, did not go away.

I felt very strange as if I was prey to something sinister. Was someone out here in the woods besides me? I felt an unexpected chill come over me but it wasn't the cold from the night air. I glanced to my left and then to my right expecting to see something. I couldn't see anything but branches and tall bare trees for miles. I turned my head behind me and just a few feet away, I saw a tall dark shadow standing between a thick of trees, watching me. I stared and by the light of the moon I could make out the figure of a man.

At first I thought it was someone walking the woods like myself, someone from a nearby cabin. Once I fixed my eyes on him, I noticed he had no features. He had no face! He was completely dark, blacker than the night and darker than the trees in the woods. But I could see him, a tall dark shadow and he could see me. What was I looking at? My mind was swimming in search of answers and my heart started to thump faster and harder. I felt uncomfortable and scared, but more than that, I knew I was in danger. Then the sudden realization that the figure started to walk in my direction, paralyzed me. His gait seemed to quicken and with each deliberate step he was **getting**

44

closer. The strange thing was I couldn't hear footsteps or twigs breaking as he walked. Not a sound. But he was quickly approaching and I started to back up and then turned and moved quickly through the woods on the left bank, away from this thing.

What was it? My head tried to wrap around the strange image and understand what I had just seen. There were still many trees before reaching the pathway. Up ahead I saw something step from behind a tall crooked tree. As I approached, I could make out arms and legs, it was a man. At first I thought it was my boyfriend and I sighed with relief. But as I neared, he stepped out from the trees and I saw it was another dark figure, completely dark, jet black from head to toe, a shadow man. Not even the moonlight illuminated him. I couldn't make out any facial features, or description of clothes or anything at all. He was solid black and stood more than six feet, tall thin and sinewy standing only a few feet away from me. I stopped in my tracks trying to process in my mind what I was looking at and where he had come from.

This was not a man; this was a strange and sinister entity. I felt very threatened by the figure and my heart beat so hard I could hear it in the stillness of the night. Now there were two tall shadows out in the darkness and I desperately searched for an escape. But I didn't know my way in the woods.

I glanced in the distance for the line of cabins. Then in desperation, I unexpectedly changed my direction and darted deeper through the dark woods, not recognizing anything or knowing if I was going further away from the cabin resort. I could feel one of the shadow men following me so I picked up my pace and before long, started to run across the wooded brush in a different direction on a path that looked worn and familiar. I quickly regretted having gone out on my own. Why had I ventured so far into the woods? By now my heart beat so hard, I thought it was going to come out of my chest.

Finally through the last line of trees in the woods, I could make out our tiny cabin in the distance. I could feel the shadow man only a few feet away. I turned back and could see him gaining on me.

He was so close I thought he was going to reach out with his long entangled arms and take me with him into the dark of the woods. As soon as I left the last line of trees, I tripped on a discarded log but somehow managed to balance myself to keep from falling. I must have been running pretty fast because I burst in the door and almost fell on the floor of our cabin. I quickly locked the front door and ran to my boyfriend's arms. He was startled and knew instantly that something was wrong, my body was shivering uncontrollably. I had never been so frightened in all my life. I told my boyfriend about the dark face-less figures in the woods and my terrifying account. He comforted me and held me tight listening to my story. I'm not sure if he believed me, but I know that what I saw that night was not of this world. The shadow men I saw that night were not human. I'm not sure what they were, but I know they were evil. I do believe they are still there hiding in the woods, waiting, waiting for someone to pass by, to catch them in the dark. The worst part of it all is that the shadow man almost got me!

Karen Beckham told me her story and described the terror she felt trying to escape the evil entities lurking in the dark of the woods. According to Ms. Beckham, she has not returned to the lodge and is convinced what she saw in the woods that night was not human.

Haunted Town

T WAS A COOL OCTOBER AFTER–
noon when my parents dropped me off at
my aunt's house in a small town outside of
Beaumont. My grandfather's illness had turned for
the worse and he had been taken to the hospital. My
parents were driving all the way to Mexico to see him,
in hopes his condition would be stabilized. Although
I begged to go with them, they said that with the
severity of grandpa's illness, they might be gone for
several days. I was disappointed but I tried to make
the best of the situation. It was already settled, I would
stay with my elderly aunt who lived alone and had no

children. I was 15 years old at the time and thought my folks should have left me alone at home.

"I'm old enough to take care of myself, I don't need a babysitter," I grumbled.

But I didn't argue with my parents, they had a lot on their minds. I could tell by the expression on his face, my father was worried about his dad, so in resignation I waved goodbye to my parents as they drove away.

What was I going to do here? It was Friday in a strange place where I didn't know anyone. My aunt must have seen me sulk and she suggested I walk towards downtown.

"There are things to do there and it's just a few blocks away, you might find some kids your age."

After I unpacked my bag in the small guest room, I thought it might be interesting to look around my new surroundings. The town was quaint and there was some activity but not much going on for someone my age. I was curious and began to check out the town square. Many small stores lit up Main Street as soon as the sun set behind the hills.

The early evening was crisp and I headed past shops and toward the plaza. Several people were out and about and seemed to have things to do. The park was pretty, but except for some small kids playing soccer and a few lovers walking by, there wasn't too much to get excited about. In the distance I could see a football stadium so I started to walk towards the hill in hopes of catching a local game. After several blocks, I noticed it had gotten dark and the few streetlights that dotted the way offered some illumination. It was farther than I had anticipated and after twenty minutes, I found myself looking up at the gigantic stadium ahead looming over the town, impressive in size and construction.

It was a brisk walk with still a couple of blocks away, but after some minutes I heard the cadence of drums. "A football game," I started to get excited about the prospect. The stadium stood on the hill like an overbearing giant but as I got closer, I could hear the roar of people shouting from the stands. It sounded like a packed stadium as if the entire town had shown up for the game. The marching band with its loud trumpet section and drums mixed with the cheers of the crowd was intoxicating. I wanted to be with them, to be part of the fun and it didn't matter that I didn't know which teams were playing. The night was young and the air was electrifying. I could tell the game had already started, the crowds yelled loudly and I started to walk faster toward the sounds. Except for the stadium lights, the surroundings were pretty dark. It sounded like a thrilling game and the thought of being around other kids was a great alternative to moping around at my aunt's house.

I rushed toward the entrance to the south side of the stadium at the top of the ramp. Then I spotted a crevice. I checked the pockets of my pants for loose change and I pulled out a few crumpled dollars. Maybe I could sneak in or blend with the crowd. It didn't seem to matter too much to me at the time, even if I had to pay the entrance. It would be worth it. The crowds were cheering wildly and the band played in rhythm. There wasn't anyone around when I noticed the crevice was just big enough for me to peak my head inside to get a glimpse of the game going on inside.

As soon as I peered through the opening, suddenly without warning, the stadium lights shut off and the crowd went silent. What? I was standing at the stadium by myself in complete darkness! Everything was quiet except for crickets chirping in the night. What happened? I looked around. There was no one there. In fact, there was nobody at the stadium. I was standing alone in the front of an empty colossal building. I know I couldn' t have imagined the sounds or the lights. Where did everybody go? I stood completely stunned at the abandoned stadium. Was I hallucinating? I was completely bewildered and I must have stayed there staring at the stadium for several minutes before I headed back into town.

Eventually, I made my way to my aunt's house. She looked up at me, smiling from her knitting as she sat in her favorite sofa chair when I told her I had gone into town to check the sights.

"Auntie, I asked nonchalantly, "was there a game at the stadium?" She looked at me funny for a few seconds, her expression was odd.

"No, definitely not, ever since that terrible accident several years ago, nobody has used the stadium." After an awkward silence, she began to tell me a story. She explained to me with sadness in her eyes.

'It was a big game in the 1940's and football players from a neighboring town had played at the stadium. They won the championship game, but on the way back to their school, it stormed that night and the bus crashed near the bridge miles outside of town. The bus fell several feet below into freezing water. Sadly, all the players were killed. As a matter of fact, tonight is the anniversary of that tragic event.'

My aunt was completely serious, shaking her head at the tragedy. I was dumbfounded and goose bumps surfaced on my arms reminding me of what I had just been through. What had I experienced? Had I walked into another dimension? I clearly heard people cheering and there was definitely a football game going on. There were lights at the stadium. I was not on any medication or any drugs, so I know I didn't imagine it. What happened to me? Is it possible that on the anniversary of the championship game, I had heard the ghosts of a football team from years past, who returned to relive their last victory, their last moments? The incident I kept secret all my life and did not relay it to anyone until now. It is still hard for me to talk about what I experienced, but it still haunts me to this day.

Rudy Reyna told his story to me over the years and he never changed the details or the strange events that took place in the haunted town. He is convinced what he experienced in the small town outside of Beaumont, Texas all those years ago, was paranormal and an unexplained phenomenon. "I can't explain it, but it happened to me and it was very real."

Ghost
In The Bedroom

*T*HE   NE*I*GHBORHOOD   WAS shaded by the many oak trees that lined the old brick homes on the street. Except for the occasional laughter of kids playing outside, my house was quiet. It was in the fall of 1996 in November. My small family had already settled after several months in the house off Greenville in old Dallas. Everything seemed to be conveniently close to home, including the Elementary school where I taught, located only a few blocks away. Eddie, an only child and one of my former students lived further down Greenville Avenue. Once he discovered where I lived, he'd walk to my house frequently to play with my kids especially on weekends.

One Saturday, Eddie came over for a visit. I told him my children were out with their father running errands so they probably would be gone for a while. He looked a little disappointed, but I let him inside and he chose to hang around hoping they would return soon to play with him. He followed me down the hallway as I picked up after my children and began straightening their rooms. Eddie trotted at my heels as I collected laundry and toys from the floor. I walked into my bedroom dropped the clothes in a hamper and reached for my hair brush sitting on the antique dresser. I offered to take Eddie to the lake to feed the ducks after I finished my chores and his eyes lit up. I knew his mother was still working and wouldn't get home for a few more hours.

As I brushed my hair in front of the antique dresser, I couldn't help but notice Eddie kept looking behind me when I spoke, and then bring his gaze back to me nodding his head respectfully. He got very quiet as his eyes looked away as if he was watching something and then he would redirect his eye contact with me. He did this a number of times but I didn't think too much about it at the time. His behavior was of a normal 10 year old, perhaps a bit restless because he wanted to play with someone that Saturday morning.

It was a beautiful afternoon when we drove to Bachman Lake later that day. My children had not returned with their father, but Eddie was no longer bored. Families were scattered throughout the park and children played tag as parents cooked on the grills. I had bought some fried chicken on the way. Eddie and I settled at a nearby picnic table overlooking the lake. Eddie seemed to be distracted and unusually quiet, not like his usual self. Finally he spoke up.

"Miss, can I tell you something?" His eyes looked serious as the small wrinkle at the bridge of his nose made a frown. He harbored a worried look on his young face.

"Sure, what is it Eddie?"

He remained silent for a few seconds as if he had a secret and wasn't sure whether to divulge it or not. He seemed to gather his courage and finally stammered.

"Well, when we were inside your house···I ah···I ah saw something." I looked at him and tried not to show fear.

"Remember when you were in your bedroom brushing your hair?" He continued. "Well, there was someone right behind you." My skin went cold.

"What do you mean?" I asked.

"It was a little boy. I saw a little boy around four or five years old kneeling on the floor playing." He.···he··· was see through.···I mean, I could see right through him." Eddie looked puzzled.

"What was he playing?" I asked trying to remain cool and not show too much concern.

"He was stacking toy blocks on top of each other. They were not made of plastic··· they looked like they were old wooden blocks with letters."

I asked Eddie to describe the little boy. He went into detail about the color of his red jumper with suspenders, a haircut of straight blondish hair with bangs.

"Did he look at you? Did he look at me?" I asked. Eddie shook his head.

"No he just kept playing with his wooden blocks. He didn't seem to notice us. I could see him for several seconds almost a minute and then he faded and disappeared."

I had not told anyone that my daughter Karen had seen a little boy ghost sleeping in Jimmy's bunk bed just a few months earlier. Eddie's details seemed to fit the description of the little boy that had frightened Karen back in September, the night of Jimmy's birthday. After our spontaneous picnic, I took him home and Eddie never brought up the strange incident again. The ensuing months were uneventful and Eddie's paranormal account became a distant memory. His experience was something I pushed to the back of my mind.

As the school year came to a close, I invited my students to dinner at a local restaurant. It was Friday and the promise of dinner together with their teacher was all my students talked about on the last day of school. It was a neighborhood restaurant and a wonderful way to celebrate the end of a successful year with my third grade students. There were pinball machines and games at the back of the family restaurant already occupied by children when we arrived.

It was a fun evening of laughter and dinner had been delicious. My students hugged me goodbye before getting picked up by their parents. I didn't want any of my students to miss out on their goodbye celebration so, for the three remaining students whose parents were still working, I promised to drive them home. It was getting late, so I gathered my girls into my white minivan which resembled a milk truck except for the maroon trimming design across the sliding door. Before too long, we were on the road when Bibiana and Maria asked if I lived close by.

"Why yes, I live just a few blocks from here," I said flatly. My home was not far from the restaurant on another street and they chimed together.

"Can we see your house?"

"It's getting late girls. By now your parents will be waiting for you at home."

"Please, please," they begged. I drove them to my brick corner house and pointed from the car.

"O.k. now you've seen it. That's where your teacher lives."

"Oh please, can we go inside···just for a little while? Please."

I shut off the engine, reluctant to take them inside, remembering some of the strange things that had occurred in the past few months. But after a few minutes I convinced myself that it would be alright and made the girls promise they could come in for only a few minutes because it was getting late and their parents would get worried. Their insurmountable curiosity of seeing the inside of their teacher's home was amusing and they jostled inside almost running into each other as they talked all at once.

The wooden floors were shiny and creaked under their small feet as they walked into the living room with the fireplace. I had left the front porch light on, and the lamps the **living** room **gave** it a cozy warm feeling. The girls looked around the dining room andkitchen and asked questions.

"Where do you sleep?" Norma asked excitedly.

"Well we have to go through the hallway and my bedroom is on the left. My children sleep in the bedroom on the right" I said laughing.

The dark painted hallway connected the two bedrooms and the small restroom was between them. I asked the girls if they needed to use the restroom before we left. As we stood for a few seconds in the middle of the hallway, Bibiana's eyes suddenly got big. She froze in her tracks with a blank stare. Then she looked at me with her almond brown eyes and dark lashes without blinking and squeezed my arm. Something had frightened her.

"What' s wrong Bibiana?"
The other students had made their way to my children's bunk beds. Norma the tallest one, sat on the top bunk laughing with Maria. Bibiana remained quiet holding on to me tightening her grip in the dark blue hallway. After a few minutes we walked back to the living room when I noticed tears in Bibiana's eyes. She could barely speak between short breaths and seemed to be panic stricken.

"What's wrong?" She stared at me for few seconds. I led her to the sofa where she sat still holding on to my left arm. "Are you O.K? Bibiana, what's the matter?" I could tell she was upset and after some prodding, she stared at me and finally spoke up.

"Some···one···someone whispered in my ear."

"What?" I asked. "What are you talking about?"

"Someone···a child, whispered in my ear." She pointed to her right ear as tears streamed down her cheeks.

"Help me." She looked up. "He said···help me."

I hugged her, patted her back and tried desperately to convince her it was probably one of the other girls who had whispered to her, when we were standing in the hallway. After all, we had entered the hallway together in a small group and everyone was in close proximity to one another before the other girls dashed to my children's bedroom.

"No" she said emphatically. "It wasn't one of them. It was a ···a boy I think. He said help me."

By this time, the other students had returned from my children's room and came into the living room where Bibiana and I were still sitting. They caught the tail end of our conversation and looked at each other confused. I told them not to worry and made light of the experience.

I didn't want Bibiana's fear to spread to the rest of them. I cracked a couple of jokes and the girls laughed, happy to be sitting in my living room with their teacher. Everyone resumed their initial excitement, except for Bibiana. I could tell she was visibly shaken.

She remained sitting close to me not letting go of my hand even for a few seconds. She was afraid and I didn't know how to explain it away, except to keep telling her everything was going to be o.k. I felt terribly guilty. Why had I brought them to my house? Giving them a paranormal experience was not part of the plan. I prayed Bibiana would not remember the incident for too long. I wondered if she had encountered the same ghostly child my own daughter had seen back in September in her brother's bunk bed. Was it the same boy that Eddie saw playing with wooden blocks in my bedroom? Who was this child? Why did he beg for help? 'Help me' he said.

My head was swimming with disturbing thoughts. The idea of living in a haunted house was not one I wanted to admit to myself. I eventually led the girls to the car and changed the subject on the way home as we talked about summer vacation. They chattered about their family plans, ice cream, popsicles and future visits to the local swimming pool. The car ride home was fairly normal and I was relieved that Bibiana eventually participated in the conversation with the rest of the girls but remained somewhat subdued. Despite the lighthearted conversation, it was clear to me that my young student had been affected by someone or something strange at my house. That night as I lay in bed, I replayed the strange events from earlier that evening. I tried to come up with an explanation at what had happened and to understand the strange incidents over the last few months but I couldn't. I couldn't explain any of it and my mind was restless.

Nothing made any sense. It took me about an hour to begin falling asleep. I pulled the covers up to my neck. Sometime in the night, I felt my son's small hands on my back reach over in a half embrace. He was cold and was trying to get warm. I smiled at the comfort of my young child cuddling in my bed. Then I suddenly remembered, both my children were spending the night at their father's house. There was no one at home but me! I quickly turned the lamp on almost knocking it over. My heart was in my throat as I pulled the covers down. There was no one there, but the indention on the sheets revealed an imprint of a small child who had only moments before snuggled next to me.

"The house off Greenville Avenue was my home for a few years and while I lived there, many people who visited experienced unexplainable events. I did some research and found there had been a family and a boy who lived there decades before me in the 1960's. Was this the ghost boy that my daughter and Eddie had seen with their own eyes? It's been a number of years since I lived in the brick house on the corner off Greenville, and the ghost who haunts the property continues to be a mystery." (Selinda Hart)

The Landscape Ghost

IT WAS AROUND JUNE OF LAST summer when my brother started working for a landscaping company. Adrian had been on the job for only a month when he got the call. The home office sent him to the house of a regular customer who lived on the south side of town in the outskirts of San Antonio. Driving in the company van, Adrian wasn't familiar with this part of town and he was alone. The area was remote. "Man I'm out in the boonies," he whispered to himself. All he could see were trees and a few scattered houses and miles of fields.

Adrian was sure he had missed the turn when he finally found the country road. There were only a few houses and the road came to a dead end. "Ah here it is," Adrian was relieved to see a man waving at him standing in the front yard. The old man walked slowly and motioned for him to follow him inside. Adrian thought it was odd that he had led him inside his home instead of to the backyard. Instead, he pointed to a heavy looking credenza in the living room. The man wanted him to move it to the back wall. Looking at his slight frame, Adrian knew that the owner would not have been able to budge it. Adrian was glad to help and the old man was grateful. Adrian followed him toward the kitchen and he was led to the back door to begin working on the backyard.

He worked all afternoon removing weeds and pruning various parts of the garden. Adrian could tell that for the most part, the yard had been well taken care of in the past. This was his last job for the day and Adrian was glad to be on his way home. The next day the manager received an irate call from a woman.

"Why did you landscape our yard? I already had cancelled services." The manager was somewhat confused.

"Mam we received a call from your address to come out and do some work yesterday. '

The woman said that was impossible and demanded an explanation. She insisted she had not called the landscaping company and stated she wasn't going to pay for services. The manager scratched his head.

"Well, mam you already paid us."

The woman was upset and adamant insisting neither she or anyone else had called the landscaping company. She demanded to see proof of payment. Adrian returned that afternoon to the house and handed her the check. The lady stared at the personal check for a long time, her lips parted and her eyes watered. She remained silent for several moments as she returned the check and then looked at Adrian in disbelief. There were tears in her eyes.

"That's my father's check, that's his signature. I uh, I don't understand···How can this be? My father died three years ago."

Adrian learned that after his passing, the woman found it hard to continue the maintenance of the yards and eventually cancelled all services from the landscaping company. But she confessed her father was especially proud of his garden. She told Adrian, he had done a beautiful job and the garden looked like the way her father had it when he was alive. She said when she returned from work, she thought it was strange to have found the credenza moved to the back wall where her dad had it originally.

My brother Adrian, once a hard nose skeptic, left that afternoon a believer in the paranormal. There was no doubt in his mind, he had spent an afternoon with a ghost. And he still had the check to prove it!

This paranormal account told to me by Nikki Sifuentes, (Adrian's sister) is a recent one. According to Nikki, although her brother Adrian was shaken by the landscape ghost, he continues to work at the company.

Night Visitor

I HAD BEEN TRANSFERRED TO another town. The company had relocated me into a one story brick house with a small tree in the front yard. I was excited to embark on this new chapter in my life and the house was strategically close to my workplace. A family had previously occupied the house and had recently moved out. Other than the cat scratches left by their pet on the bottom dining room curtains, the house did not have a lot of wear. It wasn't long before I realized however, there was something wrong with my home. I was still living out of boxes and I had only the essentials available to me. My days were long and by the time I got home, I was completely exhausted. I'd often eat, shower and fall asleep on the coach.

One night, I had a strange dream; someone was watching me sleep. It was a man in his 70's who watched me sleep as he leaned over me from the arm rest of the couch. He was an elderly gentleman with a scowl on his face. I couldn't make out the features but it looked like he was angry. I quickly dismissed the strange dream. On the third night, the temperature in my room dropped several degrees. I awoke shivering. Had a cold front come in during the night? I coughed and the smoky vapor emitted from my breath startled me. Something was wrong. First of all it was icy cold in the room. More importantly, I felt as if someone was watching me. Had someone broken in? I sat up.

From the corner of the tiny bar in the den, a grey mist was slowly making its way across the room. I wiped my eyes making sure I wasn't imagining things. By now I was wide awake. The foggy mass seemed to move with a purpose. I was immobile and the thick mist drifted right through the front door. I got up and followed its movement and opened the front door of my house. There was no one there. But that wasn't what surprised me the most. Outside, the air was warm and still. It was only cold inside my house. I checked the thermostat but the air conditioner wasn't even on! I couldn't explain the chill in the room.

As the weeks passed, I settled into the house and eventually got myself a bed and moved into the bedroom. One night, I heard footsteps coming from another part of the house and leading to my bedroom door. There was a rustling sound coming from the living room. Rats? The sound stopped and I made a mental note to call an exterminator the next day. I got up to get some water from the kitchen. As I left my bedroom, my eyes adjusted to the darkness. When I walked outside the door, I stopped in my tracks. Something was standing at the end of the hallway. It was a dark figure. My heart started to pound. Then the figure quickly moved away from the entrance. My hand scrambled to turn on the light. I walked into the living room expecting to catch the intruder. There was no one. I looked everywhere and I didn't have much furniture so there weren't too many places he could hide. The fact is there was no one in the house. What was going on in my home? I wasn't dreaming or hallucinating. I know I saw a dark figure of a man. I didn't know who to ask or what to do about this strange happening. Eventually things settled down and I forgot about it. Several months later as I was sleeping in my bedroom, I started to have the strange dream again. There was someone watching me and my heart started to pound in panic. It startled me so much, I awoke. I glanced to the right of my bedroom and saw something coming out from the dresser mirror. It was the dark figure of a man. He strategically maneuvered himself on to the floor like a slithering snake. The strange night visitor was very black, darker than the night. He turned his face to where I lay and he stood at the foot of my bed. I couldn't make out eyes or any facial features at all. But I knew he was staring at me. I was lying in bed completely paralyzed. Then he started to walk toward me. I was so shocked, I couldn't even open my mouth to speak. My mind raced and I started to think fast and remembered the Lord's Prayer.

Suddenly and unexpectedly a blue light from the bathroom window came on. The alley is situated several yards behind my bedroom and bathroom. I don't know if it was a car driving by or what had caused the blue light to come on. But as soon as the light entered from the window, the dark figure turned away from the light and walked right through the closed bedroom door and out of my room. What had I just seen? It wasn't long before I moved out for good. I was never a believer in the paranormal and I thought ghosts were simply a figment of someone's overactive imagination. I no longer scoff at people who claim to see ghosts. I never found out who or what was haunting that house. But I wasn't going to stay and find out. Whatever it was, I'm sure is still there.

This account shared by R.G. Benson took place in 2010. Benson no longer works for the same company. He has since gotten a job in another city and is living happily in a house with no paranormal activity. But he says, he still wonders about the apparitions and the unusual entities occupying his former home.

Agnes

I WAS EARLY OCTOBER, AND as a fourth grade teacher I was determined to have a successful year in my new assignment. It wasn't uncommon for me to stay in my classroom to check papers and prepare for the next day. Maybe it was all the time I spent after hours, but it didn't take long for me to figure out there was something very strange going on in the old school. The building was built in 1924 and the pipes often made clanking sounds. The floors and the stairs creaked and it wasn't unusual to hear noises coming from the ceiling and long hallways. There was comfort in my solace however, and eventually I grew use to the late hours and the strange sounds of the school. Sometimes Angela the custodian would come by to check on me. She'd finish cleaning all the classrooms in her wing, and peek her head in to say hello. She was a welcome sight and her visit gave me a nice break.

One Friday evening, Angela came to my classroom earlier than was customary during her shift. She said hello almost inaudibly, her expression was serious and I couldn't help but notice something was wrong. She looked a little pale and was unusually quiet.

"Are you O.K.?" I asked.

She smiled and asked, "Miss, are you going to stay a little longer? I'm thinking of closing up tonight."

I glanced out the window. It was dark outside and I knew it was pretty late, but she normally stayed until 10:00 p.m.

"Well, I'm almost finished, is there something wrong?" She looked at me for a few moments, not sure whether to divulge her secret.

She whispered, "I uh···think I···saw a ghost."

I stared at her and realized she was not joking.

"Wha···Where···?" I followed her to the second floor.

My mind raced wildly. What if an intruder had broken into the school? Angela explained she was in one of the classrooms on the first floor when she heard footsteps climbing up the stairs. She followed the sound all the way to the old wing. Then she noticed the footsteps stopped outside room 205. As she entered the classroom, she heard the ruffling of papers. She didn't see anything out of place and just as she was about to leave, she noticed a woman sitting in the corner at the teacher's desk. Angela stopped what she was doing and stared in disbelief.

"The woman looked transparent, she seemed to be sorting papers or something. She didn't look at me at all," Angela blurted. "It was the strangest thing, then she just stood up and walked across the room. She disappeared into the wall!"

I looked around the empty classroom and saw nothing unusual. This was the oldest part of the school and the walls had many tiny cracks and chips of paint coming off. The room had several windows facing the courtyard and rows of trees below.

"Are you sure it wasn't a reflection?" I asked trying to convince myself of a logical explanation.

I knew that the classroom faced the playground. If the room had faced the teacher's parking lot, I could dismiss it to the head lights of a passing car. But there weren't vehicles or anything with lights coming from the playground.

"Oh no, Miss it was a woman···a teacher, I think··· She never looked at me. She just got up from that desk over there and walked through the wall. I could see right through her."

I remained quiet and tried not to let it scare me. As we walked down the stairs, we passed the first floor hallway.

"Look Miss, that's the woman!"

I froze, expecting to see an apparition. But Angela was pointing to a portrait hanging on the wall. The painting was of Agnes Cotton, the name of the former teacher and principal for whom the school was named after. It was believed that Agnes' older sister had painted her when she was a young woman and the portrait, now in a frame hung outside the library. I had seen the picture many times on my way to Faculty meetings or whenever I was in this part of the building, but never paid too much attention to it.

The simple portrait had a small brass plate underneath with the name "Agnes Cotton."

The next day during a lesson I walked toward my desk and turned on the "Elmo", an updated overhead projector. I wanted my students ready and told them to expect similar operations on an upcoming exam. The Elmo was one of my favorite and recent additions of technology to my classroom of twenty two students. I utilized it well and liked to show examples of word problems and go over multiple steps of problem solving. During instruction, I had just stepped away from the Elmo for a moment and continued talking about the key words to highlight to help them with their process, pointing to the screen behind me on the wall.

Suddenly I saw the eyes of my students open wide in awe and almost immediately I noticed they were staring at something. They looked stunned, their mouths gaped half open in surprise. I turned around and saw the arm and hand of a woman on the screen. It looked like a woman's blue sleeve and hand moving left and right under the light of the Elmo for a few seconds. It was of a young person, her hands looked like that of a girl. But there was no student standing by the Elmo. Then suddenly without warning, the image disappeared.

My students started talking at once and several asked aloud, "What was that? Whose arm was that?"

It wasn't my hand under the Elmo as I had walked away during my lesson to the middle of the room. Everyone including myself had witnessed the very strange phenomenon. I didn't know what to say or how to explain to my students what we had all just seen on the screen only moments before.

Later that evening after I packed my teacher manuals and stuffed student papers in my teacher bag to go home, I passed the library. I glanced at the wall and stopped in my tracks to look at the portrait of Agnes Cotton. It was the innocent face of a girl no more than 16 coming of age. But what struck me, was the blue blouse with long sleeves she had on in the portrait. Could it be? Was it her? Had Agnes Cotton herself showed herself to my students **and me** ? Was she being curious with the technology that didn't exist in her time? I am convinced it was the same blue sleeve and young hand I had seen earlier. Agnes Cotton had made her presence known in my classroom to all my students and their teacher. I believe her ghost still roams the halls of the school.

Based on teacher Ms. Fernandez's true account, "Agnes Cotton Elementary continues to have paranormal activity. Other teachers have also heard ghostly footsteps on the second floor and doors slamming when no one is in the building. It is believed the activity increased when recent renovations began at the school. No one ever stays late at school because of all the scary things. We don't want to run into Agnes."

Birthday Surprise

THERE WAS ST*I*LL A LOT OF cleaning to do, but I was committed to getting my little house as spotless and presentable as possible. My son Victor Jr. would be arriving that afternoon and I wanted everything to be perfect. I hadn't seen him since Christmas and was beside myself with excitement. He told me over the phone yesterday, his plane would arrive just in time for my birthday. I couldn't stop whistling and smiling ear to ear. I had already mopped the kitchen and dusted the furniture. My congestion was a minor annoyance and my allergies were acting up, but other than that, I felt quite well.

"Mom, don't overdo it," shouted my daughter Liz from the other room.

"Just the living room," I yelled back. "I'm almost finished. The carpet should be vacuumed.

I was pleased with myself. It was still early and by the time Victor arrived, the house would look nice and remind him of the home he knew as a child. He was now a successful businessman living in Chicago and although he lived far from home, he was a good son and called often. Victor always came home for my birthday and had kept his promise all these years ever since he was promoted and had been transferred to the Chicago office.

"Mom, let me do that, rest it's your birthday," my daughter called from the kitchen. But by the time, she walked in I was almost finished. I had kept my pace up and ran through the entire room with the vacuum cleaner. I was content with the appearance of my house.

"The living room is the first room everyone notices," I told her.

I glanced at the clock; it was 2:00 in the afternoon. My body was feeling warm and I was unusually tired so I decided to lie down for a few minutes.

"Mom, are you O.K?" Liz asked, worried when she saw me lying down on my bed.

"Just a little tired," I said smiling. "Let me rest for a few minutes, I'll be fine."

After a short nap, I sat up and felt dizzy. The room was spinning and my head was throbbing.

"Oh no, I hope I'm not coming down with something," I whispered to myself.

I didn't want to worry my daughter and at the same time I didn't want to hear her say "I told you so," and scold me for overdoing the house cleaning.

My throat was burning every time I swallowed. I shuffled to the kitchen and reached for my cinnamon in the top cupboard of the kitchen. The best thing was to make some tea. I had the house to myself. Liz must have gone to run errands and I knew she'd be picking Victor up from the airport soon.

"My lemon tea should take care of everything," I said aloud.

Sipping from my oversized cup, I rested the back of my hand across my forehead. Trickles of sweat outlined my brow and hairline, I was running a fever. Quietly, I walked back to my bedroom, careful not to spill my tea. I knew Victor would be here in a few hours, so I decided to rest and pray my symptoms go away. The last thing I wanted was to be sick on my birthday. I didn't want my daughter or my son to see me this way and I certainly didn't want them to get sick. I fell asleep soon after drinking my tea. When I awoke, my symptoms felt worse and I could barely open my eyes. Everything was a blur. My eyes were watery and my eyelids were heavy. I felt Victor sitting next to me.

"Victor!" I said excited with my hoarse voice, "your home."

We embraced for a long time and I could smell the sandalwood and musk from his cologne.

"Happy Birthday," he whispered in my ear. I recognized the scent. It was the same one that his father wore when he was alive. It made me smile. He lay me back down and covered me with the bed cover.

"Ssh" he said. He knew I was sick and wanted me to rest.

By late afternoon a couple of hours later, I sat up refreshed. My fever had broken and I felt better. What happened? How could I have gotten so sick? I must have overdone it with the cleaning, and the excitement of my son's visit had gotten me all worked up. When I got up from my bed, I felt energetic and well. I was relieved to be back to myself. When I walked in the kitchen, Liz was sitting at the counter.

"Where's Victor?" I asked.

"Mom, he's not here yet. His plane arrives in an hour. Actually I'm leaving right now to the airport."

"What are you talking about?" I was with him just an hour ago. He gave me a big hug and wished me a happy birthday." Liz gave me a puzzled look.

"Mom, no one has been here. What are you saying? I just spoke to Victor. He called to remind me to pick him up at gate 5. He'll be here in an hour. I still have his text with the information of the name of the airline and flight number."

"No, no I saw him," I insisted. "He was sitting at the edge of my bed. I even smelled his cologne," I laughed. "Do you know he uses the same one your father use to wear when he was alive?"

Liz stared at me and I got quiet for a few moments. I suddenly realized who had come to visit. It was   my deceased husband Victor. He was a loving and caring man who prided himself in always being the first one in the household to wish me a happy birthday. His passing last year was hard on all of us. But his cancer had spread and we knew he only had a few months to live after he was diagnosed. My dear husband Victor must have seen how sick I was feeling and came to look in on me. As was his custom when he was alive, he still wanted to be the first to wish me a happy birthday.

This paranormal account and true story was told to my mother by her good friend Angie. She described the events of her birthday surprise and a visit from her dearly departed loved one.

Who's Been Playing
With My Kids?

I *WAS LATE AUTUMN AND THE*
trees that dotted our old neighborhood had
started to change into their red and gold coats.
My children were looking forward to dressing up in their
Spiderman and princess costumes for Halloween. But it
wasn't for another week. As for me, I was busy trying to
fix things and do small repairs around the house. The
lights were always going out and I was convinced it was
due to poor electrical wiring and the house being very
old. I lived alone with my two small children and I didn't
want to frighten them, or maybe I didn't want to scare

myself. They were so young and innocent; I didn't want to give in to the notion that something strange was going on ever since we first moved here. Thank goodness they were oblivious to the creepy sounds and strange happenings in the house.

My children were very creative when they played. They often made up games to entertain themselves, but recently I noticed they had started to set a third place at the kitchen table.

"Who is sitting here?" I'd ask. They would just giggle. When they played they would divide their toys into three equal parts.

"Who is coming over?" I'd ask. "No one" they looked at me puzzled.

I thought they were just acting like normal kids so, I didn't think too much about it. On more than one occasion, I could have sworn I heard a different voice amidst my children's playing, especially when they talked to one another. I didn't recognize the voice chatting with Karen and Jimmy, but it sounded like another child. Was I hearing things? It wasn't unusual to hear my name being called, "mommy." It had already happened a few times.

I'd distinctly hear "mommy" from the other side of the house and once I appeared in my children's room, they swore they had not called me and looked at me strangely. Were they playing tricks on me? I would scold them, but they looked confused, reassuring me that they had not called me.

Once, when I had come in from the back door of the kitchen, I heard a loud "mommy!" It was urgent and sounded like a call for help and I ran to my children's room thinking something had happened. I looked inside at the empty room and suddenly remembered, my children were not at home, they were visiting their father for the weekend. I was standing alone at the entrance of the children's room. There was no one there, but I know I had just heard a child calling for his mother. I walked in their room and glanced all around me, trying to explain the voice of a child. I was quiet for a few minutes, thinking perhaps I had heard children playing outside and had been mistaken. But I know I clearly heard "mommy" and it sounded like it had come from inside the house from my children's room. The yellow brick house with its cracked foundation and creepy sounds was home to our small family and I didn't want to move again. I had invested all my money into this house and I liked the fact that it was close to my workplace. But something was going on in my home and the strange experiences were becoming too frequent to be mere coincidence.

One night, it was unusually windy outside. My children had gone to bed and I walked in their room to kiss them goodnight. Karen slept soundly on the top bunk bed and my youngest Jimmy was already asleep in the bottom bunk bed. I covered them with extra blankets anticipating a cold night. I could already feel the chill in the room.

"This house," I whispered and shook my head. "It's always cold in here."

I retired to my room and could hear the wind howling and picking up outside. It wasn't long before I fell into a deep sleep. I dreamed of a huge rock wall, then like an aerial camera zooming out, the pillory in the center of town was revealed. A woman's head stuck out encumbered by the long bolt or wooden bar that also held her arms. The time period looked like Colonial America. Or was I in Salem at the time of the infamous witch trials of 1692?

I felt the shame and the discomfort of the person being held for public viewing. Then I realized, the woman in the pillory was me!

The next thing I remembered was a little girl with reddish brown hair dressed in a long dark dress with a top white collar at the end of a long narrow hallway. She wore a little white cap tied under her neck. I tried walking to her, her face looked sad and abandoned. I recognized her immediately as my daughter. But she wasn't my daughter Karen, from this lifetime. Somehow, I just knew she was mine. She extended her arms to me, but the harder I tried to reach her, the longer the hall got. I was desperately running down this long never ending hallway. She was standing at the end with open arms. I couldn't reach her and a feeling of desperation and great sadness engulfed me.

Then from out of nowhere, a sinister low menacing evil voice whispered in my ear.

"She's mine." My heart started to pound hard. Paralyzed with fear, I was aware that I was in in my room, unable to move or open my eyes.

It was as if someone or something was holding me down hard on my bed. The sinister voice was breathing in my ear and I knew immediately, it meant me harm. I was not dreaming, I could clearly hear his words and feel the breath on my ear. I knew I was in my bedroom and conscious of my surroundings. But as much as I tried, I couldn't open my eyes and was completely immobile. The low breathing continued and then I heard it, a man laughing in my ear. The strange male voice started to say obscenities. I tried to ignore it and unable to move or cover my ears, I started to pray the 'Our Father' in my head and then verbalized it saying it over and over and louder and louder until the voice started to fade as if it had been pulled away from me. But before it left, it threatened me again in a loud whisper.

"She's mine···They're mine."

Oh my God, my children! I broke from the grip that held me down, and sat upright reciting the Lord's Prayer aloud.

Trickles of sweat lined my forehead and hair. I sat up, my heart was pounding out of my chest, then I raced in my socks to my children's room trying not to slip over the cold wooden floor. I stopped myself in front of their bunk beds. They looked like little angels asleep, they were so still. I stared at my daughter for several seconds breathing as if I had raced a marathon and then I stared at my son. Thank God, they were alive, breathing normally and sleeping serenely. They were safe, for now. I have never felt so threatened in all my life. What was this entity, the one who had threatened me? Why did it want my children? I realized my children were at risk with this thing and it seemed to be living in my house. Then I stopped and wondered in horror, "Who had been playing with my children?"

My children and I experienced scary things that could not easily be explained at the house off Greenville. Although I dismissed many sounds and things in the beginning, other visitors to my home also experienced strange paranormal activity. After a while, I couldn't deny it anymore. We lived in a haunted house!

Hotel Ghost

IT WAS JUNE 16TH, 2011 AND WE were set for a lazy day at Galveston beach. My husband and I plopped down on some lounge chairs under a huge umbrella and planted our bare feet in the sand. It wasn't long before a man wearing a t-shirt with the words BEACH BUM written on it came to charge for the rental. He overheard us talking about our stay at the Tremont. The young man suddenly turned ashen.

"Did you say the Tremont Hotel, the one located on the Strand in Galveston Island?" he asked with concern.

"I use to work there. Oh, but I suppose you've already heard all the stories."

"What stories?" I asked curious.

"Well that the hotel is haunted," he said in a serious tone. I laughed thinking he was joking with us. But he remained somber.

"Haunted? Why do you say that?"

"Well, during the two years I worked there, we had a lot of paranormal activity at the hotel. And I can tell you from personal experience, strange things happen there.

You know in the lobby as you come in from the front entrance, there are three pictures hanging on the wall hanging one over each other."

"Oh yes, the ship paintings," I said.

"Well, every day I worked there, we had to straighten them. You would set them right side up go about your business and in minutes they would go back to being tilted. I mean if it was one picture, it would make sense, but all three? Not a day would pass by that I wouldn't have to straighten them up and then they would go right back to hanging on their side. It was as if a ghost was taunting me!"

"Oh yes, I know the ones you are talking about, they hang near the elevator."

"And speaking of the elevator, you know the first one on your right as you enter the lobby, well that one just has a mind of its own."

My husband and I just smiled entertained by his stories. He talked about something that had happened back in the 1800's and of a traveling salesman who had won a lot of money after playing a game of cards. Apparently he returned to his room and some time before the morning, someone came to his door and shot him dead. His winnings from the night were stolen. It was fervently believed by employees of the hotel, that the ghost of the salesman controlled the elevator and he would make it open and close at will.

I laughed again and said, "Well it sounds like a good ghost story but I don't believe in ghosts.

"Maybe the management likes to perpetuate the story to entertain the guests," I said with humor. He shook his head.

"Uh, I don't think so. Most people I know don't want to stay at haunted hotels."

Then he asked us if we remembered seeing the enormous palm tree in the middle of the lobby.

"Yes it's huge, impressive···almost touches the ceiling."

He described several occasions in which certain guests got unexpectedly brushed by a falling palm leaf.

"It happened several times. No one is ever hurt, but a large palm leaf falling from a high altitude would always startle the chosen guest. Management would do their best to appease them.

"I tell you, it was like having a prankster ghost at the hotel!"

My husband paid him for the beach chairs and umbrella and we relaxed all day forgetting about the ghost stories. That evening after dinner, we made our way back to the Tremont. I saw the huge beautiful palm tree in the middle of the lobby that reached several feet up in the air. I smirked to myself thinking of what the rental guy said earlier about the hotel's paranormal activity. A falling leaf was not paranormal in my opinion. It could happen at any time, I thought to myself. After a day at the beach and walking all day on the strand, my husband and I made our way to the elevators.

"So, what do you think about having Ghosts at the Tremont Hotel?" I snickered sarcastically with my husband.

"He was funny," my husband said. "Yeah, that guy sure has an imagination."

Just as I was about to press the elevator button, the elevator doors opened. The button was not turned on and it had not been pressed. We waited expecting someone to exit from the elevator. We both peered inside. It was completely empty.

"Ooh, spooky," I said aloud and we both chuckled. Then before we stepped inside, the elevator door started to close.

I yelled, "Wait!"

Just as I was about to press the button, the elevator doors suddenly stopped halfway and re-opened on its own. It was as if someone had stopped the elevator either from the inside or the outside. But the button was not pressed or lit. My husband and I just looked at each other and stepped inside to go to our floor.

"Hmm, must be the travelling salesman," I said in a mocking tone. We both laughed and got off on our floor.

It had been a long day at the beach and both my husband and I had strolled for hours on the Galveston strand and toured the Moody Railroad Station and various historic buildings. It had been a wonderful weekend getaway and we would be leaving the following morning. But we were tired and after a long shower, I was ready to retire to bed and just get some sleep.

We quickly fell easily into slumber. But though my room was beautiful and my bed was comfortable, my sleep was somewhat restless. I tossed and turned that night. I felt as if someone or something was watching me. It was late when I opened my eyes and glanced at the alarm clock on my stand. It was 3:00 in the morning. I tried to shut my eyes to go back to sleep, but I felt exceedingly uncomfortable. I had the strangest sensation that someone was watching me. My husband was fast asleep and my eyes slowly adjusted to the darkness of the unfamiliar room.

At the corner of our bedroom my eyesight made out the outline of a tall man. At first it was a long indiscriminate shadow. Gradually I made out a head, torso, arms, and legs. It was a man staring at me. I thought my eyes were playing tricks or that I was simply tired. But I blinked my eyes and rubbed them and I looked at the corner of the room again. It was a man with dark wavy hair that grazed his shoulders. He was dressed in a long greyish blue coat jacket. He looked like he was from a different period in time. He looked tormented and disturbed and didn't move. He wore an awful facial expression and continued to glare at me.

I opened my mouth to yell and wake my husband, but I couldn't verbalize a word. Nothing came out of my mouth, I was in shock. This was not a figment of my imagination. I lay wide awake and could clearly see a tall angry man with a scowl on his face. He started to walk closer toward our bed. I tried desperately to nudge my husband awake but couldn't move a muscle except for my eyes and I could see the strange man getting closer and closer. I noticed the strange man was focused on some-thing on my husband's nightstand. It was a wad of twenty dollar bills tied in a money clip and loose change. The man kept his eyes on my husband's money and as he got inches away from us, he slowly turned and glared at me. He was a frightening image and his deep set eyes pierced me with a horrible accusatory look. We both locked eyes for a few seconds and then he slowly disappeared, evaporating like a mist.

In the morning when we went to the front register to check out of the hotel, the concierge at the desk asked if we had a good visit. I said yes and smiled politely. After a few minutes, I spoke up.

'Can I ask you something?' I blurted trying to act nonchalant. 'Is it true that a traveling salesman was murdered back in the 1800's in this hotel?'

She chuckled and said 'well, I know that a story like that is mentioned on ghost tours, but it wasn't here, exactly.'

'So there is some truth to that story?'

'It's a well-known story around Galveston. Something took place around the late 1800's on the property next door. It seems after a long night of playing a game of cards or something of the sort, a salesman won a lot of money. His body was found dead in his room the following day and his money was stolen. Some people think it was one of the men with whom he gambled who went to knock on his door in the middle of the night. It is believed that the salesman heard a knock on his door, and when he opened it, he was shot and killed. It was a strange case and the murder was never solved."

She was quick to clarify the incident had not taken place on the premises of the Tremont Hotel.

"But nothing like that happened in any of our hotel rooms⋯ uh, why do you ask?"

"Oh no, I had just heard the story somewhere."

I didn't want to say I had seen a man from before the turn of the century in my hotel room the night before. How was I going to explain to her or anyone else I had seen a ghost? If it was the traveling salesman, he looked like he was searching for something. Was it coincidence that the money my husband left sitting on his nightstand, got the attention of an apparition? Whoever I saw that night was a restless ghost of a man who I believe continues to haunt the Tremont hotel.

The story was told to me last summer. According to my good friend Monica, "I can now say with conviction, I am no longer a skeptic and I don't laugh at anyone's stories of the paranormal. To this day, I believe a tormented ghost haunted our room at the Tremont hotel that night. The ghost probably won't ever rest until he finds his stolen money."

Cliff Of Darkness

Natalia Lizardi was born in Spain in 1901 and later moved to the States. The following is a true account of what happened to her when she was 16 years old.

THE MORNING HAD QUICKLY elapsed into afternoon as my three younger sisters couldn't talk about anything else but going into town. Our house was close to the woods, not far from the beautiful, treacherous cliffs in Costa Brava Spain. As children, my parents had forbidden us to play close to the cliffs as they were very dangerous and several people over the years had fallen to their deaths. Our cozy home was less than couple of miles outside the nearest 'Pueblo.' It was a good walking distance for my family and going into town meant going to market and possibly buying new shoes.

They could hardly contain themselves while my baby sister Theresa pulled my hand and tried to coax me to go with them. She didn't understand why I wanted to stay home. I offered to stay behind and finish the house chores, so my parents reluctantly agreed. The bustle and chatter from my sisters faded as everyone walked towards town. I secretly looked forward to having the spacious house to myself without my sisters entering the room or making noise while I tried writing my private thoughts in my diary.

The house was silent and as soon as they were out of earshot, I ran upstairs to my room and pulled my book of secrets from under a loose floor board. Writing stories and poems in my personal journal was my favorite pastime. As a 16 year old girl who shared a room with two sisters, moments of privacy were scarce and precious. As I lay on my bed, rays of orange sunlight shone from the window and washed the room with warmth and quietude.

The hours passed while I lay deep in thought on my small bed, when in the distance I heard faint music. It was low at first and gradually the mysterious melody became louder as if the wind and the trees had carried it closer to home until it was almost outside my window. For a moment, I sat still listening and soon deciphered an unfamiliar beautiful piece played on a woodwind instrument. The tune was filled with musical notes in minor, compelling and mysterious in its sound. It seemed to approach until it was right below my window beckoning me to come out. Then amidst the alluring melody, I heard my name.

At first it was like a whisper, "Natalia." Someone was calling me, "Na ta li a···come." I didn' t recognize the voice but it seemed to be coming from the woods. I looked outside the window from the second floor yet I couldn't see any one. I could hear the strange soft music and a voice in the distance, "Natalia, Natalia come here." The music, mixed with the strange voice seemed to put me in a trance-like stupor. I remember staring out in the vicinity of the woods for several minutes before turning around and taking slow deliberate steps down the stairs and out the door.

"Natalia," the voice called and I obediently walked deeper and deeper into the woods. A fierce wind had blown in from the ocean. It picked up unexpectedly and swayed the tree branches back and forth in my path as I walked into the dark woods. Above, the sky looked more like night fall, it was getting late. My parents always warned us about not going into the woods alone and especially not in the dark. I knew I shouldn't be out at this time, and my parents and sisters would be returning home soon. Still, I didn't seem to have any control of myself and kept walking further into the dark woods. The voice kept calling my name and the melody was so compelling; it seemed to have a strange hypnotic hold on me.

Dark clouds had rolled in and it looked like night-time had unexpectedly descended. I kept walking toward the voice, until suddenly I found myself past the woods and a few feet away from the edge of the forbidden cliffs. How could the afternoon have turned into night in a matter of only minutes? I couldn't see very well in front of me when I suddenly stopped. In my head I heard my parent's verbal warning, "Don't go into the woods alone, stay away from the "Cliff of Darkness."

Standing a few feet away from me was the outline of a tall dark shadow. He was standing at the edge of the cliff facing me only a few feet away with the horizon behind him, and several hundred feet below were the rocks and the angry sea. I could hear the waves crashing violently and although I knew it was late, any remnants of sunlight had completely vanished.

"Who···.who are you?" I stuttered almost inaudibly.

I was met with silence. The strange figure did not answer me and I felt an empty pit in my stomach. I could not make out any features from the shadow.

"Who···are you?" My voice trembled.

I could only make out an arm raising and motioning me to come closer. I was gripped with fear and yet, I couldn't scream or move a muscle. My right hand reached for my gold medallion hanging from my neck. My finger felt the imprint of the sacred heart carved delicately in my precious heirloom that had been passed down from my grandmother. She had given it to my mother and on my 15th birthday and as the oldest daughter, my mother had given it to me. Frozen and paralyzed, I tried to recognize any facial features from this dark figure. The oncoming storm had rendered an almost pitch black night making it almost impossible to see anything. Only his eyes shone a fiery red like burning coals and I thought my vision was playing tricks on me. I kept staring as he stretched out his hand; he knew my name and his low voice called me to him.

"Come closer."

He kept repeating my name in a low baritone voice with more and more urgency. I thought my heart was going to come out of my chest, it palpitated so hard I could feel it pound with every beat. Just then, lightning lit up the sky followed by a loud thunder and at that same moment it seemed to wake me from my trance. Lightning struck again for a few seconds and I got a good look at the mysterious figure. Jutting out of his head were prominent long narrow horns that curved at the ends like an animal. His face was long and distorted; he resembled a large goat. His body was covered with fur and his legs were strange, somewhat deformed as if he was half man and half animal. I went into shock at the sudden realization, this was not a man.

What was this thing? It wasn't an animal because he could speak and he seemed to know my name. This was not a human being at all, but what was it? It was so frightening, my legs buckled and I fell weak to the ground on my knees. Paralyzed and unable to move or get up, I closed my eyes tight and placed the medallion in my mouth clenching it hard with my teeth and I began to pray fervently. I prayed and prayed.

'Our Father who art in heaven···' Over and over, I kept repeating the Lord's prayer without letting go of my medallion. My hair blew wildly with the torrent night wind lashing my face. After what felt like a long time, the wind subsided and the dark clouds eventually dispersed; then silence. I slowly opened my eyes and saw there was light in the sky again. I was still on my knees and somehow gathered the courage and energy I had left to get up. I found myself standing wobbly at the very edge of the cliffs; one more step and I would have fallen to my death. I gathered my strength and could see the water lashing violently at the rocks below. The dark menacing figure was gone.

I could tell it was dusk in the horizon when I blinked several times and gradually felt myself recover from what seemed like a living nightmare. I don't remember what happened next except my heart beat very fast and the tears welled up inside me. I found myself running desperately through the woods all the way home. Thin branches hit me as I scurried haphazardly toward home. Twigs scratched me on my face and arms, it stung but I didn't stop running. I pushed the front door open and once inside the living room of our home, I ran to my father's arms babbling and crying. The tears were still streaming from my face as I recounted what had happened to me. Everyone stared at me stunned.

My sisters were quiet at first and then burst out laughing. They thought I was playing a joke on them! To my dismay, no one believed me. My sisters and my mother said I was being overly dramatic and warned me to stop joking.

"I didn't make up the story!" I yelled and pleaded with them.

Then I remembered as I pulled out my medallion and told them how I had bitten it several times with my teeth and prayed fervently for God's help. Everyone suddenly stopped talking and stared as my mom slowly approached me and held the sacred heart of Jesus in her hands to investigate it closely. Around it, were the many teeth marks I had permanently left on the gold medallion.

Theresa Lizardi verbally relayed her story. "It has been many years since my grandmother's terrifying experience. She never saw the evil figure again but said on rare occasions she swore she could still hear music and her name being called in the distance. This occurred throughout her early years as she grew up, until she married and finally moved away from her home town and away from the woods. The story has been passed down generations in our family. I know the story to be true because I now have her gold medallion and it still has evidence of her teeth marks when she clenched it in fear before the dark and sinister figure at the Cliff of Darkness."

Bonus offer for readers of this book.

Receive a free ghost story from Selinda Hart's

private collection by visiting:

www.ghostlycreepy.net/Landing-page.html

About the Author

Selinda Hart is a teacher and freelance writer and has written for online publications as well as for the National Radio program "Tia Maria" a talk show about ghosts, hauntings, and true paranormal experiences. She earned her Masters in Educational Leadership from the Woman's University in Denton, Texas in 2004. Ms. Hart is a "Sensitive" and has worked on paranormal investigations in Texas. Her first collection of hauntings and unexplained phenomena are based on research and personal accounts as well as her own paranormal experiences.

Website: www.ghostlycreepy.net

Email: selindahart@gmail.com

Made in the USA
Middletown, DE
24 November 2015